William Parker Cutler, Ohio Historical Society

The Ordinance of July 13, 1787

for the government of the territory northwest of the river Ohio - a paper

read before the Ohio State Historical and Archæological Society, February

23d, 1887

William Parker Cutler, Ohio Historical Society

The Ordinance of July 13, 1787
*for the government of the territory northwest of the river Ohio - a paper read
before the Ohio State Historical and Archæological Society, February 23d, 1887*

ISBN/EAN: 9783337381103

Printed in Europe, USA, Canada, Australia, Japan

Cover: Foto ©Andreas Hilbeck / pixelio.de

More available books at **www.hansebooks.com**

THE

ORDINANCE

—OF—

JULY 13, 1787

FOR THE GOVERNMENT OF

THE TERRITORY NORTHWEST OF THE RIVER OHIO.

A PAPER READ BEFORE THE

OHIO STATE HISTORICAL AND ARCHÆOLOGICAL SOCIETY,

FEBRUARY 23d, 1887,

BY

HON. WM. P. CUTLER.

WITH AN APPENDIX CONTAINING VALUABLE HISTORICAL FACTS.

MARIETTA, OHIO:

E. R. ALDERMAN & SONS, PRINTERS.

The Ordinance of July 13th, 1787.

The intrinsic merits of that organic law which was enacted by the old Continental Congress on the 13th of July, 1787, "for the Government of the Territory North-west of the river Ohio," have been so fully discussed and are so well understood that any attempt in that direction would be little more than a repetition of views already familiar to an intelligent audience. Its *merits* can now be measured by its *fruits*. *Results* are its *monument* and its highest *eulogy*.

It is not surprising that as a century is rounded up, the thoughtful inquirer should look back and endeavor to trace the beginnings and look up the extrinsic circumstances as well as personalities that were connected with such an enactment.

So far as organic law is concerned we are sitting under "vines and fig trees," are "eating of the oliveyards and vineyards that we planted not." Who were the planters? Why was the planting done?

In pursuing this inquiry we are met with the difficulty arising from a lack of authentic historic material. One hundred years ago the proceedings of legislative bodies were not kept with that plethora of discussion, and detail of motions, references and reports that distinguish modern Congressional Records. The wasting processes of a century have destroyed valuable family papers, and memories of early actors and listeners have faded out, so that fragments of *fact*, *incident* and *history* must be gathered up and carefully applied. Still the gleaner must be content with a gleaner's share of the harvest.

The passage of the Ordinance at the time has one peculiar characteristic that is worthy of notice. That is the leading fact that it stands out in history as an isolated effort on the part of its authors to forecast a complete system of government and project it over a vast territory in advance of its actual occupation by future inhabitants. When the Mayflower passengers neared their expected haven of rest, they solemnly agreed to observe certain fundamental principles of a future government; but those principles were not firmly and enduringly fixed upon Massachusett's soil until the Constitution of 1780. It required 160 years to reach that advanced stage of free institutions which was foreshadowed by the Mayflower declaration. But the Ordinance of '87 was thrown forward into a wilderness, carrying with it not only organic principles, but embracing the details of a governmental autonomy that has stood the test of a century. This peculiarity is worthy of notice, because the very fact that such an organic law was forecast, pre-arranged, and pre-ordained by competent authority, prior to territorial occupation assists us in the inquiry as to its origin, and helps to explain the fact that it was largely the work of Pioneer settlers seeking homes under its protection, rather than of wise Statesmen who had no such motive to guide them.

There were two methods by which the progress of civilization moved westward from the Atlantic base. One was by the individual enterprise of the Pioneer venturing out either alone or with a few neighbors and taking possession of the wilderness in advance of civil institutions. The other was a thoroughly organized system of occupations, with pre-arranged guarantees of protection based upon law and order and combining all the essential principles upon which our Republic is founded. Now it is necessary to keep distinctly in mind that there was a systematic and well organized *plan* for taking possession of the Ohio Valley and the Northwest in the interest of an advancing Christian civilization, that the men engaged in this effort were not mere land buyers or home seekers, but that from its incipiency the Governmental idea was part of the *plan*. *They intended to found a State.* This original intendment bore fruit in the Ordinance of July 13th, 1787.

The journals of Congress, although extremely meager in details present some facts of great value in tracing out the beginnings of a public policy in regard to the Northwest Territory. Even before its acquisition under the terms of the treaty of peace in 1783 the policy of "independent states" had been announced.

After all claims of particular States had been quieted and it could be treated as common property it became a blank sheet upon which the ideas and policies then prevailing in the old Thirteen States could be indelibly stamped. There was a sufficient divergence then as now between the Eastern and Southern States to give rise to controversy. In the land system, range, town and section prevailed against "indiscriminate locations." The transition from extreme colonial and states rights to a centralized power can be traced in connection with this "common property." Social and industrial policies came into conflict. The system of forced labor which had been universal in the colonies laid claim to this new and vast area. Its advocates on every trial of legislative strength had triumphed until it was disposed of finally by the ordinance of July 13, 1787. Subsequent interest in the ordinance itself has been directed largely to the problem that of the eight States voting for it five were slave States and the ordinance contained a positive prohibition of a system of labor which at that time was zealously guarded as the basis of their own prosperity.

The subject was not a new one in Congress. More than once distinct action had been taken, and every slave State had resisted any efforts to exclude slavery from *new territory*. Even a prospective prohibition had been denied when the Resolutions of April 23d, 1784, were adopted. Subsequently a direct anti-slavery amendment was laid over without action and never called up. As late as the 9th of May, 1787, about two months before the passage of the present anti slavery ordinance, a committee having a majority from the free states reported an ordinance for the government of the Northwest Territory that was silent on that subject, showing plainly enough that all effort at prohibition had been abandoned.

What valid reason then was there that under the leadership of Virginia, the Carolinas and Georgia with Delaware should quietly give up that which they held safely in their own hands, and which had been virtually surrendered to them by their opponents? Why did Virginia lead off in discarding her own institutions and cordially adopt those which prevailed in Massachusetts? Why were New England ideas and policies enduringly stamped upon this vast interior—the very heart of the great Republic.—at a time when New England had but one voice out of eight in deciding that result?

I ask your indulgence in an effort to answer these interesting questions.

In the beginning of the Revolutionary struggle Massachusetts was entitled to leadership in the army. She yielded it to Virginia. When Washington came to the *front* as Commander-in-Chief, that *front* was in Massachusetts. He was there brought into close personal contact with her citizens and her soldiers. His first success was the evacuation of Boston by the enemy, as a result of the prompt, energetic, and decisive support rendered to his plans by a citizen soldiery. His army was destitute of ammunition and supplies. That want was supplied by the bold privateering of Whipple, Manly, Tucker, and other yankee seamen. His disasters on Long Island were offset by the skill and daring that saved his army in a retreat requiring water passages which were conducted by the sea-faring men of New England. When driven from the "Jerseys" and forced across the Delaware, he decided upon that bold effort to inspire confidence by an attack upon his enemies in mid-winter; it was Glover's Brigade of Marblehead Fishermen that guided his craft through the floating ice of the Delaware on that Christmas night, 1776. That was a service which "land lubbers" could not have performed. In all these trying and difficult scenes he was supported by New England officers and men. Strong attachments were formed. Personal associations resulted in life-long friendships. He could say with utmost sincerity— "God bless the New England Troops."

But what has all this to do with the first settlement of Ohio, or with the Ordinance of '87?

I make the following extract from a dingy, yellow piece of manuscript which I find among " old papers," written by an early pioneer to Ohio. The writer says:

" Anterior to this period—the Revolutionary war—it is probable the great
" body of the American and English people knew about as much about the
" interior of Asia or Africa, as of this western region. With the exception of
" General Washington and some other individuals, who, by being engaged in
" the war, commonly called the French war, were entitled to locate lands on
" the Ohio, it seems few or none others had the means of obtaining knowledge.
" We are told that during the Revolutionary struggle the British established
" a printing press in New York, entitled 'The Rivington Royal Gazette.' At
" a very dark and gloomy period of that momentous struggle there was a
" very large number of papers scattered by design, that gave an account of a

" treaty of subsidy made with the Empress of Russia—the ambitious Catha-
" rine—which provided that a large number of Russian troops should be
" furnished the British for their American contest; that the troops were ex-
" pected early next season. These papers with this information fell into the
" hands of the officers of the American army, and of course became a matter
" of deep solicitude.

" At General Washington's table it became a matter of discussion: ' If this
" be true, and we are driven from the Atlantic seaboard, what then is to be
" done?' ' We will retire to the Valley of the Ohio,' says Washington, ' and
" there we will be free.' This saying was carried from the officers to the
" soldiers, by them to wives, children, and friends, and thus a spirit of en-
" quiry respecting Ohio was elicited."

This fragment of history is taken from the lips of the men who
sat at Washington's table and were members of his military
family—those old veterans of three wars—the evening of whose
days were spent on the banks of the Ohio and Muskingum, and
who indulged in a veteran's right of " fighting his battles over
again."

This traditional reminiscence finds ample support in statements
made by Ramsey in his History of the American Revolution, published in 1789. After the loss of Fort Washington and the evacuation of New York city, the American forces were driven in
hasty retreat across New Jersey and only escaped capture by cross-
ing to the west side of the Delaware river. The period of enlistment of the army had expired. Whole regiments returned home
ward. With 2000 or 3000 men of a retreating, half-naked army
whose unshod feet had marked the frozen soil of Jersey with
patriotic blood, the Commander-in-Chief was compelled to look
this question of *retreat* fairly in the face. The historian says:
" Gen'l Washington about this time retreated to Newark. Having
abundant reasons from the posture of affairs to count on the necessity of a further retreat he asked Col. Reed: ' Should we retreat
to the back part of Pennsylvania will the Pennsylvanians support
us?' The Colonel replied: ' If the lower counties are subdued and
give up, the back counties will do the same.' The General replied:
' We must retire to Augusta county, Virginia. Numbers will be
obliged to repair to us for safety and we must try what we can
do in carrying on a predatory war, and if overpowered we must
cross the Allegheny Mountains.' "

From the same historian we have also another fragment of

history giving further evidence of the estimation then placed upon the Ohio Valley as a strategic base in the grand struggle for freedom and independence. As soon as the British Cabinet became aware that France was determined to aid the United States they dispatched messengers to this country with overtures of peace, making fair promises and hoping at least to divide the councils and weaken the supports of the cause. These overtures were met by Congress with a positive demand for an acknowledgment of independence or an evacuation of the country as preliminary steps to negotiation.

The following is an extract from a letter dated June 14, 1778, written as part of a private correspondence by Henry Laurens who was then President of the old Continental Congress. He says to the King's Commissioners: " You are undoubtedly acquainted " with the only terms upon which Congress can treat for ac- " complishing this good end. Although writing in a private char- " acter, I may venture to assert with great assurance, they never " will recede, even admitting the continuance of hostile attempts " and that from the rage of war the good people of these States " shall be driven to commence a treaty *westward of yonder moun-* " *tain*."

But why should Washington point out that distant region as a base to fall back upon in case of defeat? The answer is found in the fact that he had been there. He knew something of its fertility and boundless resources. As early as 1770 he had acquired titles to over 20,000 acres of its choicest lands. In 1773 he issued proposals for colonizing those lands, offering liberal terms on the old English plan of paying quit rents in lieu of purchase. In a word Washington was a *pioneer* of the *pioneers* to the Ohio Valley. The marks of his "little hatchet" can be still traced upon the first land lines ever run in the valley or west of the Allegheny Mountains. His knowledge of the country thus obtained would be readily accepted by all who were engaged in the war, whether in the army or in Congress.

It is quite evident therefore that Washington knew and his officers knew what he was talking about when he said to Col. Reed: " *If we are overpowered, we must cross the Allegheny Mountains.*" It is also evident that Henry Laurens understood the situation when he boldly told the British Ministry: "*Let the war rage on,* sooner than accept your insidious offers of a humiliating peace our people will *commence treaty-making westward of yonder mountains.*" While Lord Howe was in possession of Philadelphia he sent out the threat to Washington that he would "*drive him beyond the mountains.*"

Now let us pass from this primitive scene—this real starting point of inquiry as respects that systematic occupation of the Northwest which was the occasion of its organic law—to another period of that intimate intercourse that had grown up between the Commander-in-Chief and his veteran officers. The great conflict is over, the pledge of *life, fortune* and *sacred honor* had been redeemed. Peace with the great enemy was assured. But other perils surrounded them. The day for disbanding the army approached. But there were no "greenbacks," no "silver dollars," no "gold coins" with which to meet final payments. Washington applied to Congress. The officers petitioned that body for relief, but its authority did not protect it from insult, and it was a fugitive from the menaces of a squad of unpaid and clamorous troops. The only remedy for the army was to accept certificates of settlement—warrants upon a bankrupt treasury. They called them "*final certificates,*" and they were *final* to many of the holders, as want and hunger forced them on to the market at " one in six," as they called it, or one-sixth of par value. These old certificates must be kept in mind, for while they were "*finals* " of a 7 years' hard service, we shall see that they were the *beginning* of another and not less important enterprise.

Col. Pickering, their Quartermaster General, thus describes the condition of the Army while at Newburg and New Windsor, waiting for orders to return, penniless to their desolate homes. He says: " To hear the complaints of the officers and see the " miserable condition of the soldiery is really affecting. It deeply " penetrates my inmost soul to see men destitute of clothing, who " have risked their lives like brave fellows, having large arrears of " pay due them and prodigiously pinched for provisions. It is a " melancholy scene." Again he says: " Those brave and deserv- " ing soldiers, many of whom have for six years exposed their " lives to save their country, who are unhappy enough to have " fallen sick, have for a month past been destitute of every com- " fort of life. The only diet provided for them has been beef

" and bread—the latter generally *sour*." Such was the testimony
" of their Quartermaster, who was most familiar with their con-
" dition." In their petition to Congress the officers say: " Our
" distresses are now brought to a point—*we have borne all that*
" *man can bear*. Our property is expended, our private resources
" are at an end, and our friends are wearied out and digusted with
" our incessant applications. We therefore most seriously and
" earnestly beg that a supply of money may be forwarded to the
" army as soon as possible." (Jour. of Con., Vol. IV, p. 267.

To such a state of exasperation were those men brought that
one of their number addressed his brother officers in the following terms: " If this then be your treatment while the swords you
wear are necessary for the defence of America, what have you to
expect from peace when your voice shall cease and strength dissi-
pate by division? When those swords, the instruments and companions of your glory shall be taken from your sides, and no remaining mark of military distinction left you but your wants, in-
firmities and scars? Can you then consent to be the only sufferers
by this revolution, and returning from the field grow old in poverty, wretchedness and contempt? Can you consent to wade
through the vile mire of dependency and owe the miserable rem-
nant of that life to charity, which has hitherto been spent in
honor? If you can—go, and carry with you the jest of Tories,
the scorn of whigs, the ridicule, and what is worse, the pity of
the world—go, starve and be forgotten."

Nothing short of a most desperate condition of affairs could have
extorted such language from one officer to his fellow officers all of
whom had served faithfully through the war. I have recalled
these rugged and unwelcome historical items reluctantly and only
because they are necessary in explaining subsequent movements.

But this dark cloud in our country's history had a "silver lining."
A bright ray of sunshine broke through the prevailing gloom.
Col. Timothy Pickering, the Quarter-Master General, at this
critical period, writing to a friend under date of April 7th, 1783,
says: " But a new plan is in contemplation—no less than the
" forming of a new State westward of the Ohio. Some of the
" principal officers are heartily engaged in it. About a week since
" this matter was set on foot and a plan is digesting for the pur-
" pose. Enclosed is a rough draft of some propositions respecting

" it which are generally approved of. They are in the hands of " General Huntington and General Putnam for consideration, " amendment and addition." Again April 14th he writes: "General " Putnam is warmly engaged in the new planned settlement over " the Ohio. He is very desirous of getting Hutchins' map. Mr. " Aitken had them to sell. If possible pray forward me one." A petition was drawn up addressed to "His Excellency the President and Honorable Delegates of the United States of America in Congress assembled." The petition was signed by 288 officers of the army asking that a "tract of land bounded North on Lake " Erie, East on Pennsylvania, South and Southeast on the Ohio " River, West on a line beginning on that part of the Ohio which " lies 24 miles West of the Scioto river, then running North on a " meridian line till it intersects the River Miami which falls into " Lake Erie, thence down the middle of that river to the lake, " might be formed into a distinct government or colony of the " United States."

They ask that their bounty lands may be assigned to them in this district, and that " provision may be made for a further grant of land to such of the army as wish to become adventurers in the new government, in such quantities and on such conditions of settlement and purchases for public securities as Congress shall judge best for the interest of the intended government and rendering it of lasting consequence to the *American empire.*"

This petition was placed in General Putnam's hands who addressed a letter to General Washington asking him to present it to Congress. Washington presented to Congress, urging it upon their attention, and subsequently " exerted every power he was master of" to secure a compliance with the wishes of his associates in the army.

Colonel Pickering drew up a plan for organizing the new government which embraced the following: " The total exclusion of \ slavery from the State to form an essential and irrevocable part of the Constitution." This was the first distinct proposition for the exclusion of slavery Northwest of the Ohio ever publicly presented or discussed and was a part of the original plan ultimately matured in '87—5 years later. It must be borne in mind that these men were not dealing solely with land purchases or their bounties. They were intent upon a " new state westward of the

Ohio." They tried their hands at Constitution making from the start. Putnam's "letter" outlined a valuable governmental policy in the West. Pickering's " plan " embodied organic principles.

We thus find that the same class of men who ate at Washington's table when the ugly question of surrender or retreat was discussed are again taking counsel together over this " Ohio scheme." *Then* the Ohio was a base for *retreat*—now for an *advance.* By the failure of Congress to act upon the petition the scheme was delayed but not defeated. The urgent necessities of the principal movers compelled them to disperse as soon as the army was disbanded and seek employment. Putnam took a contract to survey ten townships for Massachusetts in her province of Maine. General Tupper another of the signers of the petition, accepted a vacancy made by Putnam's retirement from the United States Surveyors appointed to run out the 7 Ranges. But in 1786 they met again. Putnam could say from personal observation of Maine—" That country in general is not fit for cultivation, and when this idea is connected with the climate a man ought to consider himself curst even in this world who is doomed to inhabit there as a cultivator of the lands only."

Tupper, returning from a visit to the Ohio in 1785, could say— " The lands in that quarter are of a much better quality than any other known to the New England people; that the climate, seasons, products, &c., are in fact equal to the most flattering accounts that have been published of them."

With this addition to their stock of knowledge as to locations, they issued on the 10th day of January, 1786, a paper headed " *Information*," calling a meeting of those who wished to take an interest in the " Ohio scheme " of settlement. This resulted in the organization of the " Ohio Company of associates " on the 3d day of March following.

This company, composed almost entirely of the officers of the army, decided to make a purchase of as much land in that part of the western country that had been indicated in the officers' petition of '83 as could be paid for with $1,000,000, expecting to use bounty warrants and public securities in payment. This meant the conversion of those old "Final Certificates" into future homes "westward of the Ohio." It also meant the foundation of a "new state." They appointed Gen. Samuel H. Parsons, one of the as-

sociates, to apply to Congress for a purchase of lands. He made
the application but it was not pressed as there was no quorum present at the time of his visit to New York. The views of General
Parsons as to location differed from those of the Directors, so that
another agent, Dr. Cutler, was appointed. He reached New
York on July 5th, '87, found a quorum of Congress present and
set about his work immediately. From his private journal kept at
the time we are able to trace the progress of his efforts and place
a fair estimate upon the influences that surrounded the whole subject at that time. The first subject to claim his attention was the
organic law that was to govern the future inhabitants of the country he was commissioned to purchase.

That subject had been in the hands of Congress for a long
period prior to this application for purchase of lands. The idea
of "new states" or "distinct government" was first acted upon in
Congressional proceedings on October 10, 1780, although Maryland had called their attention to the subject in May, 1779. Before
the war the same idea had matured into a grant not fully consummated by the British crown for establishing a colony west of
the Allegheny mountains. The petition of the officers was probably the first subsequent movement in the same direction *outside*
of Congress. As the Ohio Company were really consummating the
object of that petition it became a part of the duty of their agent
to look after the laws and constitution that were to govern the
country.

In all this they would be acting in harmony with the known
policy of the general government on that subject.

It must be borne in mind that the whole treatment of "vacant
territory" at that time was a change from the policy that had generally prevailed among the colonies prior to the war. As a general
thing land had not been regarded as a source of revenue to any of
the colonies or states. The British crown reserved quit rents and
fixed six pence per acre as the measure of revenue. The Virginia
plan fixed two cents per acre and threw open her lands to "indiscriminate location." No cash revenue was derived from the lands
of Kentucky, Tennessee or West Virginia.

To state the causes that led to the adoption of a different policy
by Congress and the steps taken to bring that policy into effective
operation would trespass too much upon the time of this occasion;

but it is quite obvious that if they expected to treat vacant lands as *property*—as a source of future revenue—it was indispensable to organize a government for the protection of that property as well as the purchasers. So that when the agent of the Ohio Company went to New York it was just as incumbent on him to look after the organic law as to make terms of purchase.

When he got there Ohio was a wilderness without law. Some surveys had been made under guard of United States troops, but there was no protection to families or property. This view of the matter brings up the strong contrast as to the consideration of an organic law by statesmen and politicians—however wise and justly esteemed in other matters—but who had no expectation of making a personal application of governmental principles, as compared with a body of intelligent, cultivated, refined men and families who expected to " become adventurers," as they termed it; that is to leave all, risk all, endure all that lay before them in that far off and savage country. Members of Congress did not expect to do this. Before this agent of the associates started from home he had engaged over 100 of his friends and neighbors to go, and he expected at that time to go with them. How did he find matters at New York? Congress was offering to sell some of the 7 Ranges, but nothing that could be called a government, suited to the wants even of a pioneer population had been extended over the country. In one form or other the subject had been before them since its first introduction in 1780. More than twenty different members of Congress had been appointed on the various committees that during this long interval had the matter under their supervision. This labor had brought forth the resolutions of April 23d, 1784, and a reported substitute presented a few days before his arrival, probably resulting from General Parson's application for lands. With some valuable principles they were mere skeletons; incomplete outlines as compared with the Ordinance of July 13th.

By keeping in mind this inchoate state of legislation on the subject and the urgency of motive that controlled the applicants for a land purchase we may estimate the *reasons why* an organic law which has commanded universal admiration was promptly matured and unanimously adopted.

In dealing with Congress the agent was sent without limitations or instructions. In fact his own views coincided fully with his associates.

In presenting his business before Congress he has left us some records as to the lines of policy upon which he based his application. The following extract from his journal indicates the extent and comprehensiveness of his views. He communicated his plan to Mr. Osgood, President of the Board of Treasury and we are thus furnished with a cotemporaneous estimate of its value. "He "(Osgood) highly approved of our plan and told me he thought "it the best ever formed in America. He dwelt much on the ad- "vantages of system—said system had never before been attempt- "ed—that if the matter was pressed with spirit he believed it would "prove one of the greatest undertakings ever attempted in Amer- "ica. He thought Congress would do an essential service to the "United States if they would give us the land rather than our "plan should be defeated, and promised to make every exertion "in his power in our favor." Such an estimate from such high authority could only have applied to the organic law as well as the mere purchase of land—the two combined making *the greatest undertaking ever attempted in America.*

Here is an evidence that he understood his mission to be the founding of a future Commonwealth. This accorded fully with the declared policy of Congress as well as the design of the originators of the scheme. The "associates" were nearly all officers of the army—men of experience, intelligence and correct principles—but they selected their agent from another calling in life. True he had served as Chaplain in the army, but his life and labors had been identified and spent with that remarkable class of men known as the "New England" or Puritan clergy. They were as a body *remarkable* because at that time and previously they exerted a greater influence in shaping the character and giving direction to the active energies of a whole people than any other class of citizens. They had carefully considered and constantly presented to the people the essential principles of human rights, of personal liberty, of the necessity of obedience to law, in a word all the firm foundations upon which a Republic can stand. As a support to these principles they had organized and maintained a system of popular education, extending from the common school to institutions of highest culture. Their influence over the people resulted from *religious convictions*. That influence flowed from Puritan pulpits and permeated every fiber of social, civil and political life. They were the founders and guides of a *people's conscience*. They were not politicians—did not claim to be statesmen. Yet governmental institutions were moulded by their precepts.

Ramsey, in his " History of the American Revolution," fully supports this view of the prevailing influence of the clergy at that time. He says, (Vol. 1, p. 199), "The clergy of New England were a numerous, learned, and respectable body, who had a great ascendency over the minds of their hearers. They connected religion and patriotism, and their sermons and prayers represented the cause of *America* as the cause of *Heaven*."

To their influence may be traced those moral and educational principles that are a distinguishing feature of the Constitution of Massachusetts and other New England Commonwealths. It is only a fair inference that one of their number should improve the opportunity to insert the same ideas and policies into an organic law which was to protect his family and neighbors in their future homes.

The agent left his pulpit temporarily to undertake the important service assigned to him. He was compelled to deal with governmental questions—questions too which Congress had failed satisfactorily to solve. *Land* was of no value to him or his associates without *law*. He was seeking homes for intelligent, cultivated Christian families. If then he acted at all—if he suggested or advised it must be in a line with his life-time convictions. A New England clergyman would not forget or discard that which was equivalent to his own identity—*his principles*. As a matter of history we find that after his arrival in New York he spent several days in constant intercourse with members of Congress before he entered fully upon negotiations for the purchase of land—that the governmental ordinance was submitted to him—that he suggested changes that were adopted. Giving then a proper weight to these preliminary considerations, his agency in preparing, and procuring the insertion in the Ordinance of July 13th of Freedom, Civil Rights, Religion, Morality, and Knowledge, which are its distinguishing characteristics can hardly be questioned. It is well supported by traditional evidences. It is also supported by the fact that in his land purchase subsequently made he secured for the benefit of settlers in each township a section of land for both schools and religion, and two whole townships for a university; and also by his subsequent personal efforts to promote those important objects.

These principles and policies were just the foundation that himself and associates desired upon which to build *their own future homes.*

This much is due to the "truth of history" in throwing light upon a subject that has not been well understood.

It remains to consider some reasons why the views of the agent were so fully and unanimously accepted; why Congress gave promptly all that was asked for.

It was incumbent on him to procure for his constituents, "the associates," the best terms practicable for safely prosecuting their scheme of settlement.

But decisions rested with the sovereign power in Congress assembled.

As we look back over the transaction, the prohibition of slavery occupies a prominent place in popular estimation. At that time it may be doubted whether it was entitled to that prominence.

The principal object of the Ohio Company certainly was not to abolish slavery northwest of the river Ohio. It was in their way and they simply brushed it out of their way. They wanted the best principles of civil liberty and social order all supported by morals and education, and they secured them. But they had broader views even than these. They had taken the dimensions of the American Empire. They regarded the Northwest as its heart. They forecast its immense resources and planned for their future growth and full development. A brief notice of the situation as it then existed is necessary to give proper weight to the reasons that controlled Congress in yielding to the Ohio Company substantially all they asked for.

I have traced the connection of Washington with the "Ohio scheme" up to the disbanding of the army. In his farewell address he reminds his companions of their prospects in the west in the following words: "The extensive and fertile regions of the west will yield a most happy competence to those who, fond of domestic enjoyment, are seeking for personal independence." Sparks, Vol. 8, p. 483.

We have also the positive statement of the Directors of the Ohio Company entered upon their Records in the following words: "The path to a competence in this wilderness was pointed out to us by the Commander-in-Chief of the American Army." There can be no doubt therefore that the initial steps of this organized system of settlement of the Northwest, embracing fully, States, governments, laws and constitutions, had been carefully matured as between the New England officers, with whom personal contact had been maintained throughout the war, and their Commander-in. Chief. But there is further evidence of the identity of interest which grew out of those personal associations.

Washington's personal relations and activities to the Ohio Valley had just begun. Immediately on resigning his command of the army he undertook a tour of observation through western New York, evidently with an eye to its commercial advantages, then a six week's trip to the Ohio Valley. On his return to Virginia he addressed himself to organizing efficient lines of commercial intercourse between Virginia seaports and the Ohio Valley and the lake region. He sought from General Butler, then Indian Agent, a solution of this problem of water communications between Lake Erie and the Ohio River. He accepted the oversight of a chartered company for the improvement of the Potomac. In a long letter to Governor Harrison, of Virginia, he discusses with great intelligence the true commercial interests of that State as connected with the fertile west and urges action to secure its trade and retain its loyalty to the Union by the "cement of interest."

In a letter to David Humphreys, dated July 25, 1785, he says: "My attention is more immediately engaged in a project which I think *big with great political* as well as *commercial consequence* to the States, especially the middle ones. It is by removing the obstacles and extending inland navigation of our rivers to bring the States on the Atlantic in close connection with those forming to the *westward* by a short and easy transportation." (Sparks, Vol. 9, p. 114.) He thus marks out a National line of policy in regard to internal improvements. All this was an object of vigorous pursuit and of earnest prosecution by Virginia statesmen at the time of the application of the Ohio Company to Congress. In a pamphlet published by Dr. Cutler, after his visit to New York, designed to give information about the West, he discusses the same topics that were engaging Washington's attention. He foretells the use of steamboats on western waters; Washington refers to an invention of Rumsey's for applying mechanical powers to boats. Both discuss the question of *carrying*, *places* or *portages* between the Atlantic rivers and the Ohio and the Lakes. There is abundant evidence that the productions and commercial values of the great West were at *that time* understood, appreciated and thoroughly canvassed by the intelligent managers of the Ohio Company and by Virginia statesmen. Evidences of this harmony of views and interests can be found in the following sources of information: 1st, the pamphlet prepared by Dr. Cutler in 1787, and his other writings. 2d, a letter addressed by General Putnam to Fisher Ames in 1790, discussing the question whether the West was worth retaining in the Union. 3d, Washington's letter to Governor Harrison, and other letters written by him on that subject after his resignation from the army and prior to his election as President of the United States.

In these papers, all worthy of a place among State documents, the true situation of the west at *that time*, the views of all parties, their expectations, their plans, the motives that controlled their decisions are all presented and fully discussed. From this hasty sketch it must be evident that when the Agent of the Ohio Company appeared before Congress he could look for friendly co-operation from one source outside of any connected with his company. That source was Virginia and Virginia statesmen. I know of no evidence that General Washington exerted any direct influence favorable to the plans of his old military comrades, except as I have already stated, but he was earnestly, ardently engaged in promoting plans that would be greatly enhanced in value by the permanent occupation of the Ohio Valley, adjacent to his own lands, by an industrious, intelligent and enterprising people. His lines of water transit would be of little value without products for a commerce. It is but reasonable to claim that Virginia statesmen were interested in the same way. Accepting then the situation as it then stood, we have an explanation of the fact that the agent went directly to Virginia and " members from the Southward," and placed his business in their hands.

The Carolinas and Georgia might well be supposed to say to Virginia, " This Northwest is too far removed from our borders to make it a matter of essential interest to our States. If you can secure protection to an exposed frontier from Indian depredations; can invite industry and good neighbors, and can control commerce from a vast interior. If the army in this way can receive a benefit we will yield our objection to the prohibition of slavery, and will accept that which promotes your prosperity without injuring us."

When the agent of the associates started on his mission to New York for the purpose of purchasing lands in Ohio he took numerous letters of introduction, and among them, to Carrington, Grayson, and Lee, members of Congress from Virginia, from their old military comrades—Parsons and Putnam—Directors of the Ohio Company. This was like a reunion of old veterans.

The Virginia Congressmen could sympathize with the wants and wishes of their companions with whom they had served through the great struggle. This accounts for the fact that a new Committee on the Governmental Ordinance was formed with Carrington as chairman, Lee as a member, Grayson being temporarily President of Congress, and at all times a leader in all that pertained to the western country. He thus alludes to these three Virginia members, "Grayson, R. H. Lee, and Carrington are certainly very warm advocates." " Mr. R. H. Lee assured me he was prepared for one hour's speech, and he hoped for success."

All this looks like a cordial and hearty response to the wishes of old comrades in arms, and that Virginia interests were involved in the result. If we had Lee's " hours' speech," and the tenor of the many conferences held between the agent and " members from the Southward," especially the Virginia delegation, the reasons would be disclosed why *slavery* quietly stepped down and out and gave place to the coming empire of freedom—*Religion* and *Knowledge*.

I have thus endeavored to assign to causes known to exist at the time, their proper and legitimate weight in determining questions of great importance as connected with the first settlement of the Northwest and the formation of its organic law.

I do not regard the exclusion of slavery as resulting from a sudden fit of philanthropy or as solely due to personal views on that subject. With the Associates its positive prohibition was a "sine

qua non"—so also were the principles of civil and religious liberty
with the supports of morals, religion and knowledge. The trouble
with Congress was that while they had a well defined policy of
establishing "new states"—"distinct governments," they failed in
providing an organic law suited to the class of men who proposed
to occupy the territory. This want was supplied by one who had
received the training of that body of men who had a most intelligent view of civil, social, and political rights, who were intimate
with the real wants as well as remedies of the masses and had
carefully studied the problems of law, order and right, in all their
applications. While he availed himself of all cotemporaneous influences to accomplish his mission, the essential elements that were
necessary for the foundations of a commonwealth were at his
command, and he managed to throw them forward in advance of occupation over a territory designed for *Christian
homes.*

He secured the consent of Virginia and other Southern States
for a transfer of New England principles, policies and industrial
customs to a new and virgin soil. It was a happy blending of important business interests with correct governmental principles all
combining to secure unanimous approval of a grand result.

By tracing, thus hurriedly and imperfectly, these preliminary
steps we are brought to that crisis in our Nation's life that is char-
acterized by Mr. Bancroft in the following language: " Before
" the Federal Convention (then sitting in Philadelphia) had re-
" ferred its resolutions to a committee of detail, an interlude in
" Congress was shaping the character and destiny of the United
" States of America. Sublime and humane and eventful in the
" history of mankind as was the result it will not take many words
" to tell how it was brought about. For a time wisdom and peace
" dwelt among men and the great Ordinance which could alone
" give continuance to the Union came in serenity and stillness.
" Every man that had a share in it seemed to be moved by an in-
" visible hand to do just what was wanted of him; all that was
" wrongfully undertaken fell by the wayside—whatever was
" needed for the happy completion of the mighty work arrived
" opportunely and just at the right time moved into its place."
Yes, it came quietly, in "serenity and stillness," for in eight days

a problem was solved that had occupied the attention of Congress for eight preceding years.*

From this view of the personal influences and extrinsic circumstances that surrounded the beginnings of our Organic Law, we may turn for a moment to one of its important characteristics that was shaped by those surroundings.

The articles of the Old Confederation were little more than a treaty between thirteen independent States, and were formed to meet the exigencies of the contest with the mother country. The weak point was the inability of Congress to enforce taxation as a basis of *public credit.*" This weakness very early drove them to the vast real estate contained within the bounds of the Territory Northwest of the river Ohio, as a basis for a credit resting upon common property that could be used for common benefit. In very many different resolves and reports " vacant territory " or the " back country " is referred to in this light. The numerous appeals made to the States to surrender all claims, so that the title might rest absolutely in the United States rested upon this ground. As early as September 5th, 1782, a proposition was submitted to regard these lands as a means of paying the " debts of these States." Mr. Witherspoon moved an amendment so as to use the words " *National debt* " instead of the " debts of these States." With the claim of common proprietorship grew up the theory of unity of control, or a complete sovereignty, vested in the United States in Congress assembled over the territory, both as property to be disposed of for common benefit, and as territory to be governed by a supreme power. Witherspoon threw, as it were, a mustard seed of *nationality* into the virgin soil of our institutions.

On the 24th of April, 1783, Madison, Ellsworth, and Hamilton, in a report, refer to the " national debt," and state their reliance for its extinguishment to be " vacant territory." On the 13th of September, 1783, Mr. Carroll, of Maryland, offered a proposition asserting that " the United States have succeeded to the sovereignty over the western territory, and are thereby vested as one undivided

---

*On the 2d of May, 1779, the Delegates from the State of Maryland received instructions that were entered upon the journals of Congress, claiming that "the unsettled country if wrested from the common enemy by the blood and treasure of the Thirteen States should be considered as common property, subject to be parceled out by Congress into free, convenient and independent governments in such manner and at such times as the wisdom of that Assembly shall direct."

and independent Nation, with all and every power and right exercised by the King of Great Britain over said Territory." This sounds like a *declaration of Nationality*.

On the 5th of April, 1784, a grand committee of one from each State report, " that Congress still consider vacant territory a capital resource, and this too is the time when our Confederacy, with all the territory included within its limits, should assume its ultimate and permanent form." When the resolutions of April 23d, 1783, were under consideration, Mr. Read, of South Carolina, offered a proposition that the settlers should be governed by Magistrates appointed by Congress and under laws and regulations as " Congress *shall direct*."

None of the above propositions were adopted by Congress. They only show that there was a *sentiment* of *nationality*, and that it gathered around the Northwest Territory.

It was a plant of slow growth. The Land Ordinance of May 20th, 1788, distinctly recognized a separate ownership of each State in the western lands, and provided that most of the deeds to purchasers should be made by Loan Officers of the several States, and the purchase money paid to them. The resolutions of April 23d, 1784, contained a very feeble assertion of the absolute right of the United States to govern the inhabitants of the territory; but the Ohio Company went directly to the United States in Congress assembled, made their purchase of land from the Board of the Treasury, and on final settlement took their deed from George Washington, President. This was the first complete assertion of sovereignty by the United States over the " vacant territory " *as property*. The same is true as regards the Governmental Ordinance. The reasons for this must be found in the peculiar wants, views, and policy of the Ohio Company in dealing with Congress. They could not carry out their plan by buying in the 7 Ranges, because in that case they must deal with thirteen different owners and accept alternate townships or sections of land. They wanted a tract about equal in amount to all the 7 Ranges, and they wanted it in a compact form.

Then again their views of Governmental principles were not satisfied with anything short of a supreme authority so lodged and regulated as to command *obedience to law*. They wanted *order* as well as *law*. At that time the authority of the Confederacy sat very lightly upon the pioneer settlers who had pushed their fortunes into the great west.

Washington said to Governor Harrison of Virginia: "The West stands, as it were, on a pivot—the touch of a feather may turn it any way." The views of the Ohio Company were very positive on this subject. Dr. Cutler makes this entry in his journal during his negotiations with Congress: "The uneasiness of the Kentucky people with respect to the Mississippi was notorious. A revolt of that country from the Union if a war with Spain took place was universally acknowledged to be highly probable; and most certainly a systematic settlement in that country, conducted by men strongly attached to the Federal Government and composed of young, robust, hardy and active laborers who had no idea of any other than the Federal Government, I conceived to be an object worthy of some attention." General Putnam subsequently discussed very fully with Fisher Ames the question: "Can we retain the West in the Union?" and asks only protection to ensure its loyalty. The Associates had no idea of any other than the Federal Government, but they wanted that Government to assert its sovereign rights in an Organic Law that would protect them from any wild scheme of disunion that might be sprung upon them.

There is abundant evidence that the location, at the right time and at the true strategic point of such a body of true and loyal man, with whom Washington's wishes and policies were law, had much to do in controlling and defeating incipient steps toward disunion, in turning the "pivot" in the right direction. With these views on the part of the associates it was essential to them that the Organic Law should assert those rights and powers that are national in their character. The company, through their agent, pledged a full support to governmental authority in advance. The result shows that both as regards land as property and territory as the subject of supreme governmental authority, there was in connection with this transaction as full an assertion of nationality as circumstances would permit. All this was really outside of any distinct authority conferred upon Congress by the articles of Confederation.

In that transition period from a jealous adherence to State Rights to a full acceptance of national sovereignty, this was an important step taken in advance of the fully matured assertion of the same principle in the Constitution. The influence of this advanced step in deciding the formation and adoption by the States of the Nation's Organic Law cannot be traced with accuracy, but the men who secured from Congress this assertion of power outside of the articles of the Confederation were all ardent friends of the Constitution—then in process of formation—and it is not unreasonable to suppose that the land sale with the Governmental Ordinance had an influence in the right direction. Eight States were committed to the principle of nationality, and a large and influential body of citizens were thus pledged to its support.*

Another feature of the Ordinance is worthy of notice as connected with Dr. Cutler's negotiation for a large purchase of land.

The Ohio Company had no charter, although it was the intention of its originators to procure an act of incorporation from one of the States or from Congress. The land purchase was therefore a *private contract*. The following provision in the Ordinance may be regarded as a full equivalent for a public charter: " That no law ought ever to be made or have force in said Territory that shall in any manner whatever interfere with or affect private contracts or engagements *bona fide* and without fraud previously formed."

That Dr. Cutler regarded his land purchase as a *private contract* is very evident from an entry in his Journal, Oct. 26, 1787, when

---

*The following is an extract from a letter written by Richard Henry Lee to General Washington dated July 15th, 1787, two days after the passage of the Ordinance. He says: "I have the honor to enclose to you an ordinance that " we have just passed in Congress, for establishing a temporary government " beyond the Ohio, as a measure preparatory to the sale of lands. It seems " necessary, for the security of property among uninformed and perhaps licen- " tious people, as the greater part of them who go there are, that a strong- " toned government should exist, and the right of property be clearly defined." Mr. R. H. Lee was Dr. Cutler's friend, who promised an "hour's speech" to aid him. It is quite evident that a "strong-toned government" for the west was fresh in his mind two days after the passage of the Ordinance. He assigns the "uninformed and perhaps licentious" character of the people as a reason for such a government—referring to settlers already there—not to Dr. Cutler's proposed band of emigrants. Dr. Cutler refers in his journal to the same uneasy condition of Western affairs and proposes as a remedy a colony of men of a different character and who were strongly attached to the Federal Government. This coincidence of views between Mr. Lee, who undoubtedly represented the prevailing view in Congress, and the agent of the Ohio Company shows clearly enough that a " *strong-toned government* " grew out of this systematic plan of settlement.

he paid over $500,000 to the Board of Treasury. He says it was "the greatest private contract ever made in America."

Mr. R. H. Lee refers to the Ordinance, "as a measure preparatory to the sale of lands. It seemed necessary for the security of property * * that a strong-toned government should exist and the rights of property be clearly defined."

The strong presumption is that this valuable provision as well as others relating to "rights of property" were suggested by Dr. Cutler as a protection to his property in the absence of a charter..

I have thus hastily passed over the ground from which sprung the elements of the first settlement of Ohio and the Northwest, and have assigned reasons why some of the distinctive features of the Ordinances of '87 were inserted. I have done this solely in the interests of the *truth of history*—not to advance claims unsupported by facts—but to award to every actor in the important labors of that primitive period their full and just credit for work so well done.

It may be claimed that the true thread of history may be traced in the course of that "Providence that guides our ways," and *our nation's ways*, "rough hew them as we may," beginning with the early knowledge of the Ohio Valley obtained by the man who, as Commander-in-Chief, was detached from his native associations, thrown early in the Revolutionary struggle with New England men, imparting to them his own observations, then pointing out to them a "competence" in the western "wilderness," as an alternative to the humiliations of poverty, that he undertook on behalf of his native State a broad and comprehensive scheme of internal improvements, resting upon Virginia seaports as one terminus, and covering the Ohio Valley, the Lakes and the Northwest, combining the highest motives of patriotism with a most intelligent appreciation of commercial results. That there was in all this a perfect harmony of interests, a coincidence of views, a co-operation of effort as between Virginia statesmen and the Ohio Company that readily accounts for the unanimity of consent in accepting freedom and discarding slavery. It is also evident that the religious, moral and educational forces that for a previous century had been growing strong, resolute and well prepared for activity and most important service in New England, were skillfully and successfully transferred to this Western Empire by that organized and systematic method of settlement which marked its beginnings on the banks of the Muskingum on the 7th of April, 1788. Massachusetts and Virginia joined holy wedlock and Ohio was their first born. The ordinance was the child's cradle. All this looks like a chapter in the "*Romance of History.*"

It will thus be seen that *Ohio* was a star of Hope among the gloomy camp fires of Valley Forge, that the "*new State westward of the Ohio*" was a broad streak of sunshine in that dark hour of poverty, discontent and dissolution at the close of the great struggle, that an intelligent and systematic plan of planting a *new State* in perfect harmony with the policy of Congress was wisely and well matured, that cordial approval of its organic principles resulted from full equivalents to those who held the power to make decisions, that in all this there was a kindly co-operation growing out of personal associations, that a good degree of harmony as between the North and South then existed, resulting in concessions for the common good, that patriotism was the rule, and local jealousy the exception; that organic foundations were laid broad enough and strong enough to bear up the fabric of an Empire.

Standing here, as we do, upon a century's summit, looking back with reverent gratitude upon the work of its founders, we may gather in as historical results, that the 12,000,000 of people composing the five great Commonwealths now quietly dwelling upon what then was the wild surface of that old " vacant territory," may claim for themselves and their pioneer fathers, that in all the slow and tedious processes of *building up*, in cherishing organic ideas and giving them vitality, in supporting their *Nation* and moulding its character, in defending its *life* in time of *extremest dangers*, they have borne their full share of patriotic service, and may now pass that *nation* over, with a clean record to posterity, sending its ideas and principles *onward* in their mighty mission of dominion from sea to sea, and from yonder beautiful river (Ohio) to the ends of the earth.

APPENDIX I.

The original contract made by the Ohio Company with Congress was for 1,500,000 acres, for which they paid down as closing the contract $500,000. For various reasons they found it impossible to make up the remaining moiety of the same amount. The agents thereupon authorized Dr. Cutler and General Putnam to wait upon Congress in 1792, and effect such a settlement as would give the shareholders a good title to as much land at least as had been paid for. A petitition signed by Rufus Putnam, Manassah Cutler, and Robert Oliver, Directors, was presented to Congress March 2d, 1792, asking for a reduction in the price of these lands on the ground that the Secretary of the Treasury had recommended a general reduction in the price of all lands to twenty cents per acre, and a bill had already passed the House of Representatives, fixing the price at 25 cents per acre. In this petition to Congress the directors say, " that in the year 1783, a certain number of the officers of the late army—consulting the interest of the United States as well as their own—prepared a petition to Congress, praying that their bounty lands and also the bounty lands of other officers and soldiers who chose to take their lands in that quarter, might be located between the Ohio river and Lake Erie; and that they might be permitted to purchase additional quantities with the certificates they had received for their services."

This petition of the directors was referred to a committee in the House consisting of Sedgwick, Findley, Learned, Benson, and Baldwin. This committee reported a bill giving the Ohio Company as a settlement for the $500,000 already paid 750,000 acres —214,285 acres—also a tract of 100,000 acres for actual settlers;

besides setting apart section 16 for schools, section 29 for religious purposes, and two townships for a University.

This committee also reported a section in the bill giving the Ohio Company six years in which to pay for 750,000 acres more lands at 25 cents per acre, but this section was stricken out in the Senate. The donation tract was passed in the Senate by a tie vote, 11 to 11, the Vice President, John Adams, casting his vote in its favor.

In their report to the House the above named Committee say: "That the said Ohio Company laid its foundation in an application to the United States in Congress assembled by the officers of the late army, a copy of which marked number 1 is herewith presented to the House." We are thus enabled to trace to a true historic basis the beginnings of that organized and systematic plan of settlement which was consummated at Marietta, April 7th, 1788. This document number 1, referred to as the "foundation" of the "Ohio Company," is in the following words:

"*To his Excellency the Presiaent, and Honorable Delegates of* "*the United States of America in Congress assembled:*

"The Petition of the subscribers, Officers in the Continental Line of the Army "*Humbly Showeth*

"That by a Resolution of the honorable Congress passed September 20th, "1776, and other subsequent resolves, the officers (and soldiers engaged for "the war) of the American Army, who shall continue in service till the estab-"lishment of *peace* or in case of their dying in service, their heirs are entitled "to receive certain grants of lands according to their several grades to be "procured for them at the expense of the United States.

"That your petitioners are informed that the tract of country bounded north "on Lake Erie, east on Pennsylvania, southeast and south on the river Ohio, "west on a line beginning at that part of the Ohio which lies twenty-four "miles west of the mouth of the river *Scioto*, thence running north on a me-"redian line till it intersects the river Miami which falls into Lake Erie, "thence down the middle of that river to the lake, is a tract of country not "claimed as the property of, or within the jurisdiction of any particular State "in the Union. That this country is of sufficient extent, the land of such "quality, and situation such as may induce Congress to assign and mark it out "as a tract of territory suitable to form a distinct government (or colony of "the United States) in time to be admitted one of the confederated States of "America.

"Wherefore your petitioners pray, that, whenever the honorable Congress "shall be pleased to procure the aforesaid lands of the natives, they will make "provision for the location and survey of the lands to which we are entitled

" within the aforesaid district; and also for all officers and soldiers who wish
" to take up their lands in that quarter.

"That provision also be made for further grants of lands to such of the
" Army as may wish to become adventurers in the new government, in such
" quantities and on such conditions of settlement and purchases for public se-
" curities, as Congress shall judge most for the interest of the intended gov-
" ernment, and rendering it of lasting consequence to the American *Empire*.

" And your petitioners, as in duty bound shall ever pray.

"(Signed)   BY TWO HUNDRED AND EIGHTY-EIGHT OFFICERS OF THE
" June 16, 1783.   CONTINENTAL LINE OF THE ARMY."

The following is a list of 282 of the names that were signed to
the above petition, as preserved and found among Gen'l Rufus
Putnam's papers and in his hand writing:

NAME.	RANK.	STATE.
John Greaton,	Brig. Genl.	Mass.
Elias Dayton,	"	Jersey.
R. Putnam,	"	Mass.
H. Jackson,	Col.	"
David Cobb,	Lt. Col.	"
Samuel Mellish,	Lt.	"
Benj. Tupper,	Col.	"
Wm. Hull,	Lt. Col.	"
Moses Ashley,	Major,	"
Jephthch Daniels,	Capt.	"
Eban Smith,	"	"
Benj. Haywood,	"	"
Samuel Frost,	"	"
John Holden,	Lt.	"
John Miller,	"	"
Jos. Balcom,	"	"
Jedr. Rawson,	Ensign,	"
Ebenr Ballantine,	Ser. Mate,	"
A. Morrill,	Major,	N. Hamp.
Peter Claye,	Capt.	Mass.
Ephriam Emery,	Lt.	"
Josiah Smith,	"	"
A. Tupper,	"	"
J. Wales,	"	"
Andrew Sarnet,	"	
Elisha Foster,	Ensign,	"
Asa Guarce (?),	"	"
Elisha Horton,	"	"
Jeremiah Lord,	"	"
Samuel Lilley Sewall,	"	"
Nathan Goodale,	Capt.	"

NAME.	RANK.	STATE.
James B. Finley,	Surgeon,	"
Ralph Bowells,	Lt.	"
Benj. Pierce,	"	"
Joseph Williams,	Capt.	"
Samuel Whitlock (?),	Surgeon.	
Tertius Taylor,	Lt.	"
John K. Smith,	Capt.	"
Jesse Hollister,	"	
John Mills,	"	
John Stark, ·	Brig. Gen'l,	Hampshire.
Wm. Scott,	Major,	"
Benj. Tallmage,	"	Conn't.
Elijah Wadsworth,	Capt.	"
Simeon Jackson,	"	"
Aaron Ogden,	"	Jersey.
Samuel Reding,	Major,	"
Jonathan Holmes,	Capt.	"
Cyrus D. Hart,	"	"
Edmund D. Thomas,	Lt.	"
Abraham Appleton,	"	"
L—— Dalsey,	Lt. Adgt.	"
John Peck,	Lt.	"
Wm. Smith,	Ens.	"
Samuel M. Shute,	Lt.	"
Wm. M. Shute,	Ens.	"
Jas. Brush,	Lt.	"
Samuel Hendry,	Capt.	"
Benj. Ogden,	Lt.	"
Moses Sproule,	Ensign,	"
Geo. Reed,	Lt.	"
Jonas Lure,	Ens.	"
Wesel T. Stout,	Lt.	"
John Bishop,	Ens.	"
Wm. Tuttle,	Ens.	"
George Walker,	Lt.	"
Wm. Kersey,	"	"
John Newcastle	"	"
Ebenezer Elmer,	Surgeon,	"
Alexander Mitchell,	Capt.	"
John Blair,	Lt. & Pay M.	"
Wm. Helvis (?)	Capt.	"
Samuel Conn,	Lt.	"
Abner Brooks,	Ens.	"
John Holmes,	Capt.	"
Wm. Pitt,	Capt.	"

NAME.	RANK.	STATE.
Absolm Bonham,	Lt.	"
Jacob Hyer,	Ens.	"
Eph. Whitlock,	Lt. Adgt.	"
Pritchard Cox,	Major,	"
Thos. Lunsdale,	"	Maryland.
Walker Messe,	Capt.	"
Horatio Clogett,	"	"
E. Spurrier,	"	"
Thos. Rowell,	Lt.	"
Wm. Bruce,	Capt.	"
John Jones,	Lt.	"
Henry D. Chapman,	Ens.	"
Robt. Halkerston,	Lt.	"
Ezekiel Haynie,	Surgeon,	"
Wm. Watts,	S. Mate,	"
Walter Dyer,	Lt.	"
Jno. Hartshorn,	"	"
Ivory Holland,	"	Mass.
Joseph Smith,	"	"
Peletiah Everett,	"	"
Sylvanus Smith,	Capt.	"
Park Holland,	Lt.	"
Samuel Finley,	Surgeon,	"
J. Farwell,	Capt.	Hamp.
Archibald Stark,	Lt.	"
Joseph Mills,	"	"
Caleb Stark,	Lt. Aid-Camp,	"
Ebenr Stockton,	Surgeon,	"
Jonathan Perkins,	Lt.	"
Perry Ellis,	Capt.	"
Josiah Monroe,	"	"
J. Boyton,	Lt. & Adjt.	"
Nathan Meaze,	Lt.	"
Owen Bacon,	"	"
Bazaleel Horse,	"	"
Robt. B. Wilkins,	"	"
J. Cilley,	"	"
Daniel Livermore,	Capt.	"
David Allen,	S. Mate,	"
Roady Dustin,	Capt.	"
Jere Frogg,	"	"
David Gregory,	"	"
N. M. Seth (?),	"	"
John Demot,	"	"
Samuel Cherry,	"	"

NAME.	RANK.	STATE.
Lemuel B. Mason,	Lt.	Hamp.
Joshua Merrow (?),	"	"
Caleb Roberson,	Major,	"
James Carr,	"	"
Joseph Poole,	Capt.	"
Israel Euen,	Chaplain,	"
Henry Adams,	Surveyor,	Mass.
Ezra Newhall,	Lt. Col.	"
N. Price,	Major,	"
John Blanchard,	Capt.	"
Simeon Larned,	"	"
Wm. More,	"	"
D. Holbrook,	"	"
Joel Pratt,	Lt.	"
John Davis,	"	"
Olion Price,	"	"
Robt. Williams,	"	"
Africa Hamlin,	"	"
Wm. Shephard,	Ens.	"
R. S. Howe,	"	"
Moses Knap,	Major,	"
Joshua Benson,	Capt.	"
Samuel Chapin,	Lt.	"
George Reed,	Lt. Col.	Hamp.
B. Portor,	Major,	Mass.
T. Towne (?)	Capt.	"
Rufus Lincoln,	"	"
W. Miller,	"	"
Z. King,	"	"
Sam. Bradford,	Lt.	"
Luke Day,	Capt.	"
Wm. M. Kindry,	Lt.	"
James Savage,	Ens.	"
Geo. Blab,	Lieut.	"
Isaac G. Graham,	S. Mate,	"
Azariah Egelston,	Lt.	"
Ephraim Hunt,	Lt.	"
John Williams,	Capt.	"
Fredrick Freeze,	Lt.	"
Nath'l Cushing,	Capt.	"
Eben Brown,	Lt.	"
Benj. Wells,	Lt.	"
C. Marshall,	Lt.	"
Ben. M. Morgan,	Lt.	"
Samuel Lunt,	Capt.	"

NAME.	RANK.	STATE.
Joseph Fisk	Surgeon	Mass.
Adl. Warren	Lieut.	"
Benj. Jones Porter	Sur. Mate	"
Daniel Shute	Surgeon	"
Elijan Norse (?)	Lt. Col.	"
Lem. Trescott,	Major	"
Abraham Williams	Capt.	"
Wm. Torrey	Lt.	"
Hezekiah Ripley	Lt.	"
Wm. Taylor	Lt.	"
Silas Morton	Lt.	"
Samuel Myrrick	Lt.	"
Jacob Leonard	Ens.	"
M. G. Houdin	Capt.	"
Joseph Kullen	Capt.	"
Wm. Eysendear (?)	Lt.	"
Marlbury Turner	Lt.	"
Nathan Leavensworth	Lt.	"
John Hart	Surgeon	"
Joshua Danforth	Lt.	"
John Warrin	Lt.	"
Alexander Oliver	Ens.	"
Jonathan W. Grey	Ens.	"
John Burnham	Major	"
Benj. Gilbert	Lt.	"
Moses Carlton	Lt.	"
Zebulon Hooker	Lt.	"
Daniel McCoy	Ens.	"
Jonathan Felt	Capt.	"
John Yeoman	Lt.	"
Joseph Freye	Capt.	Hamp.
Asa Senter	Capt.	"
John Paterson	Brig. Genl.	Mass.
I. Brooks	Lt. Col.	"
Caleb Clap	Capt.	"
Levi Holden	Capt.	"
J. Huntington	Brig. Genl.	Conn't.
Hernan Swift	Col.	"
Jas. W. Wright	Major	"
Eleazer Gray	Lt. Col.	"
Leml. Clift	Capt.	"
Nathan Beers	Lt.	"
Ebenr. Frothingham	Lt.	"
John Rose	Surgeon	"
Joseph Clark	Ens.	"

NAME.	RANK.	STATE.
Aeneas Munson	S. Mate	Conn't.
Aaron Kaslor	Ens.	"
John Hobart	Lt.	"
Wm. Linn	Lt.	"
Stephen Betts	Capt.	"
Roger Willis	Capt.	"
Abner Cole	Ens.	"
Daniel Bradley	Lt.	"
Jacques Harman	Ens.	"
Ezra Serbis (?)	Capt.	"
Samuel Hait	Lt.	"
Richard Douglass	Capt.	"
Joshua Whiting	Lt.	"
John Trowbridge	Lt.	"
George Cotton	Ens.	"
Hezekiah Hubbard	Lt.	"
Joshua Knap	Ens.	"
Eben Wales	Lt.	"
Reuben Sanderson	Lt.	"
Silas Goodale	Lt.	"
O. Goodrich	Ens.	"
Wm. Wiggins	Lt.	"
John Noyes	Surgeon	"
Pownall Derring	Lt.	"
Wm. Wamsley	Ens.	"
John M. Buell	Capt.	"
Wm. Judd	Capt.	"
Charles Miller	Lt.	"
Lebens Loomis	"	"
Charles Fanning	"	"
Samuel B. Webb	Col.	"
Dan'l McLane	Lt. Col.	Mass.
H. Knox	Maj. Gen'l	"
John Cram	Col.	"
Wm. Perkins	Major	"
John Seiwell	Capt.	"
Thos. Knowles	"	"
Florence Crowley	Lt.	"
Nathaniel Donnell	Capt.	"
James Hall	"	"
Thos. Norse	"	"
Abigah Hammond	Lt.	"
Wm. More	"	"
John Callender	Capt.	"
Sam'l Cooper	Lt.	"

NAME.	RANK.	STATE.
John Doughty	Capt.	N. York.
Eben Huntington	Lt. Col.	Conn't.
Nath. Holbrook	Lt.	Mass.
Reuben Lilly	"	"
Eben Sproat	Lt. Col.	"
Jacob Town	Lt.	"
Cornelius Lyman	Ens.	"
R. Bradford	Capt.	"
Jonathan Ames	Lt.	"
John Hurd	Ens.	"
Robt. Oliver	Major	"
Robt. Walker	Capt.	"
J. Hill	Lt.	"
N. Thatcher	"	"
Jno. Whiting	"	"
Hugh Maxwell	Lt. Col.	"
Silas Pierce	Capt.	"
Thos. Foster	Lt.	"
Edward White	"	"
Joseph Crook	"	"
Joseph Leland	"	"
Wm. Hildreth	"	"
Francis Felt	"	"
James Bancroft	"	"
J. Baldwin	Col.	"
Edward Phelan	Lt.	"

Of the above names 156 are from Massachusetts.
34 are from N. Hampshire.
44 are from Connecticut.

232 New England States.
36 are from N. Jersey.
13 are from Maryland.
1 is from New York.

282

APPENDIX II.

The following estimate of the character of the men to whom their Commander-in-Chief "pointed out a path to a competence in this wilderness," is worthy of record and preservation.

In a letter to Richard Henderson, dated June 19, 1788, Washington says: " No colony in America was ever settled under such " favorable auspices as that which has just commenced at Mus-" kingum. Information, property and strength will be its charac-" teristics. I know many of the settlers personally and there never " were men better calculated to promote the welfare of such a " community." In a letter to La Fayette, dated Feb. 7, 1788, he says: " A spirit of emigration to the western country is very pre-" dominant. Congress have sold in the year past a pretty large " quantity of land on the Ohio for public securities, and thereby " diminished the domestic debt considerably. Many of your mil-" itary acquaintances, such as Gen'ls Parsons, Varnum, and Put-" nam; Cols. Tupper, Sproat, and Sherman, with many more, " propose settling there. From such beginnings much may be " expected."

When La Fayette visited Marietta in the year 1825, he inquired with intense interest, " Who were the first adventurers to settle Ohio? " On hearing their names he exclaimed, with much emo-tion, "I knew them well! I saw them fighting the battles of their country at Rhode Island, Brandywine, Yorktown, and on many other fields—they were the bravest of the brave—better men never lived."

Judge Burnett, in his Notes on the North Western Territory, uses the following language in regard to "the individuals compos-

ing the Marietta colony": " After having spent the most valuable
" period of their lives in the army, enduring every species of ex-
" posure, fatigue and suffering; they were dismissed to their
" homes, if they were so fortunate as to have any, with nothing
" but empty promises, which have never been realized; and most
" of them with broken or impaired constitutions. The certificates
" they received as evidence of the sums due them from the coun-
" try were almost valueless. They were bought and sold in the
" market at two shillings and six pence for twenty shillings; and
" as late as 1788, they were only worth five shillings in the pound.
" They were honorable, high minded men, whose feelings rebelled
" at the thought of living, in poverty among people of compar-
" ative wealth, for the protection of which, their own poverty had
" been incurred. Under the influence of that noble feeling hund-
" reds of those brave men left their friends, and sought retirement
" on the frontiers, where no invidious comparisons could be drawn
" between wealth and poverty; and where they became involved
" in the hazardous conflicts of another war."

Judge Burnet also states, that, " Three-fourths of the persons
who formed the Miami Company, and advanced the first instal-
ment of the purchase money; had served in the Revolutionary war."

The following is a partial list of the officers of the Revolution-
ary Army who were among the early settlers of Ohio, at Marietta:
Major Generals—Arthur St. Clair and Samuel Holden Parsons.
Brigadier Generals—Rufus Putnam, James M. Varnum, and
Benjamin Tupper. Colonels—Ebenezer Sproat, R. J. Meigs,
Robert Oliver, Winthrop Sargent, William Stacy, Joseph Thomp-
son, Israel Putnam, Archibald Crary, Silas Bent, Enoch Shepherd,
Alexander Oliver, and Ebenezer Battelle. Majors—Nathan
Goodale, Nathaniel Cushing, Haffield White, Asa Coburn, Ezra
Putnam, Anselm Tupper, Dean Tyler, Cogswell Olney, Jonathan
Heart, Earl Sproat, Abraham Williams, John Burnham, and I.
Doughty. Captains—Zebulon King, William Dana, Jonathan
Stone, Jonathan Cass, Josiah Munroe, Jonathan Devol, William
Mills, Robert Bradford, Oliver Rice, Joseph Rodgers, Benjamin
Brown, Charles Knowles, Jonathan Haskell, George Ingersol,
Elijah Gates, Peter Philips, Ezekiel Cooper, Daniel Davis, Jethro
Putnam, William James, Joseph Buck, John Leavins, Wm. Burn-
ham, Benjamin Miles. Lieutenants—George Ewing, Joseph

Lincoln, Ebenezer Frothingham,Thomas Stanley, Neale McGaffy, William Gray, and Benjamin Converse. Commodore Abraham Whipple. This list embraces 62 names, to which may be added many others of lower grade in the army than Lieutenant.

In the fall of 1790, Col. Sproat received orders from the War Department, to enlist a body of militia to protect the frontier. They were, however, discharged from service by order of Gov. St. Clair the next July. Col. Sproat repaired to the War Department, with his muster roll, to settle his accounts with the government. Dr. McHenry, of Maryland, was at that time Secretary of War. When the roll of names was presented, the Secretary looked it over, and exclaimed to Col. Sproat, " Why, sir, there must be something wrong about this roll, for every name is signed in full, not a man has made his mark." " Ho! Doctor," said Sproat, (who liked a joke), " they are all Yankees,—there's not a Marylander among them."

Of the 287 able bodied men, then in Marietta and the other settlements, 246 were enrolled on that list.

APPENDIX III.

SERVICES OF THE OHIO COMPANY IN DEFENDING THE UNITED STATES FRONTIER FROM INVASION.

When General Putnam undertook the superintending of the Ohio Company and landed with his organized force of pioneers at Marietta on April 7th, 1788, he assumed a more important and difficult task than that of opening a wilderness for cultivation and providing houses and homes for settlers.

On his way out from Massachusetts he stopped over in New York and made himself thoroughly acquainted with the real situation of Indian affairs in the Northwest Territory. He became satisfied that former treaties were not cordially accepted by the Indians as a finalty, and that he was facing a war the moment he set foot on the soil Northwest of the River Ohio. He at once undertook a system of defences at the cost of his Company. He did not trust alone or mainly to the United States troops then stationed at Fort Harmar. It was the duty of the Government to provide for the protection of their own citizens who had ventured out to improve the public Domain. But Putnam was fully aware of the poverty and inefficiency of his Government to afford the protection which his followers had a right to demand. He virtually assumed to take the place of the United States in this matter of defensive war against *their enemies*, and to do it at the cost of his company.

Notwithstanding this wise foresight on his part he indulged a hope of protection based upon the fact that Fort Harmar had already been established at the mouth of the Muskingum.

He writes to Dr. Cutler, dated Adelphi, May 16th, 1788, about a month after his arrival, " Should there be an Indian war this

" will be a place of general rendezvous for an army, so that in all
" human probability the settlement can never fail of the protection
" of government."

But he was doomed to disappointment in this expectation.

St. Clair's Treaty of '89 modified the situation somewhat, but
in '91 the storm of war broke out. Government instead of sending aid to the Marietta settlers, removed the slender protection
afforded by the United States troops in Fort Harmar, transferred
them to Fort Washington so as to protect the more populous dis-
tricts of Kentucky, and to operate to better advantage against the
great body of the Indians. Putnam placed his settlements under
Martial Law, ordered all to rendezvous at Waterford, Marietta or
Belpre, and undertook the defences of those three Forts.

In the fall of 1790, government granted an enlistment of militia
who were placed under Col. Sproat, but the following order issued
by Gov. St. Clair deprived the Ohio Company settlers of any
governmental protection :

" FORT WASHINGTON, July 6th, 1791.

" The act calling the militia for the defence of the Frontier has been found
" to be a very unavailing measure and at the same attended with a very heavy
" expense. You will therefore discharge all the parties that have been called
" out for the defense of Washington County, (except at Gallipolis for which I
" have already given orders), upon the 20th inst. But there is nothing in this
" order to be construed to prevent you from continuing either the parties now
" embodied or such others as you may think necessary, provided the expense
" is borne by the people themselves; but the United States will not defray
" any that may be incurred after that day."

This threw the entire expense of the war in this section of the
Northwest upon the Ohio Company.

In their Petition to Congress, March 2d, 1792, the Directors
represent the great hardship thus imposed upon them by being
compelled virtually to assume the responsibilities and charges of
the United States in this crisis. They say: " The great expense
" of the Company has amounted already to more than *thirty-three*
" *thousand dollars* in specie besides 100 acres of land to each
" share." They attribute this expense largely to " The hazard
" and extraordinary services of the settlers in securing their own
" protection.

" The settlers found themselves in a more hazardous situation
" than they expected. The small number of troops assigned to
" Western Territory being inadequate to that protection of the

" frontier which was neecssary to give security, the people found
" they must erect defenses wherever they sat down—that they
" must work in companies and guards must be continually kept or
" they could neither labor or sleep in safety."

The Directors entered into contract to give as a bounty 100
acres of land to those who would perform military service to *"the
end of the war."* Those Pioneer settlers had as much right to
protection from their savage enemy as the citizens of New York
or Philadelphia had from foreign invasion, and they came out de-
pending upon it.

General Putnam took this view of the matter, and in a letter to
President Washington, dated Jan. 8th, 1791, he says: " The Gar-
" rison at Harmar consisting at this time of little more than 20
" men can afford no protection to our settlements. It has been a
" mystery with some why these troops have been withdrawn from
" this quarter and collected at the Miami.

" I will only observe further that our situation is truly distress-
" ing, and I do therefore most earnestly implore the protection of
" Government for myself and friends inhabiting the wilds of
" America—to this we consider ourselves entitled."

Notwithstanding such appeals the burden of this defensive war
was thrown upon the Ohio Company. They accepted it and held
their forts through the war. The following is an exact " statement of account" as between the Company and the United States,
copied from an old manuscript in General Putnam's hand-writing,
and found among his papers:

ABSTRACT OF MILITIA IN THE PAY OF THE OHIO COMPANY DURING THE
INDIAN WAR.

1790	At Marietta for 1 month, wages and parts of Rations	$	135 03	
	Bellprie for 1 month, wages and Rations		92 00	
	Waterford for 1 month, wages and Rations		70 00	
				$ 297 03
1791	Marietta for Jan., Feb. and March		696 00	
1791	Marietta for April, May and June		839 03	
1791	Bellprie, Jan., Feb. and March		613 37	
	Bellprie, April and May		683 00	
1791	Waterford, Jan. Feb. and March		395 03	
	Waterford, April, May and June		498 00	
				3724 43
	Paid to Spyes, their Wages and Rations		878 71	
	Paid to extra Scouts and Guards		183 08	
	Paid to Surgeons, their wages and rations		229 71	
	Paid for Medicine and nursing sick		30 21	
				1321 71

To the amount of rations issued by Commissaries.$ 1729 52
To the amount of provisions furnished by Comp'y. 813 37
To amount of whiskey purchased............... 837 21
To amount of Ammunition purchased 506 68
                                                    ─────── 3436 78

EXPENSE OF FORTIFICATIONS ERECTED.

To the amount of Labour on the several works...$ 3888 13
To Lumber employed,viz: boards, brick, timber, &c. 382 39
To Black Smith work, Iron, &c................. 101 64
ToSundries,viz: nails, tin, paper, trenching tools,&c 296 68   4668 84

                                                    $13449 59

TO CHARGES MADE BY THE DIRECTORS.

1791 Viz: To Rufus Putnam................. $ 113 00
1791 To Robert Oliver at Marietta............$351 00
     To Robert Oliver, extra services and ex-
        pense 173 33
1791 To Robert Oliver at Marietta............ 90 00   614 33

1791 To Griffin Greene at Bellprie and Marietta 373 50
1792 To Griffin Greene at Bellprie and Marietta 118 50   492 00 S 1219 33

                                                        14668 92

To goods purchased and applied for the redemp-
   tion of prisoners.........................   40 00

                                                        $14708 92

Journal Page.   CONTRA CREDIT.
280 By the United States towards the pay and rations
        of Militia refunded ....$ 2549 42
215 By the amount of 970 rations discounted by Elliot
        & Williams per Governor's order............. 64 66
     By the amount of provisions, whiskey, ammunition,
        &c., &c., charged to individuals............ 743 94 $3358 12

Balance of clear expense......................... $11350 90
Journal 212. N. B.—Col. Sproat's return of Millitia, July 5th, 1790, is 246
        including officers.

Dr. Hildreth is authority for saying that the above "clear balance." "was never repaid by the United States, although justly due them."

The paltry sum of about $3,000,000—which would about represent that old "*balance*"—at 6 per cent per annum, interest payable annually up to 1888, is not to have weight in any adjustment of obligations as between this great Nation and its Founders. The lesson of their lives is beyond computation in money value to the coming generations upon whom is fast devolving the responsibility of preserving that which they founded.

Marietta is not a mendicant in demanding some suitable recognition of the services, the sacrifices and endurance of the Pioneer

Fathers.   The full cost of a Monumental Structure *has been paid in advance*.   The above exhibit is not the only one that might be presented.

But it is not alone or mainly the small band of brave and true men who were personally engaged in the first settlement at Marietta whose memories ought to be cherished and honored.   The wisdom of great statesmen, the responsible authors of Organic Laws, and the valor and endurance of that army composing the " Old Continental Line " cluster around events that culminated here.   This great Nation cannot afford to fling back upon such an ancestry the stinging taunt of the Newberg letters: " *Go! starve, and be forgotten!* "

APPENDIX IV.

The Society of the Cincinnati.

This society was composed of officers who had served during the Revolutionary War. Its object was to keep alive the memory of the war and to promote a more perfect union of the States.

There was one general society with branch societies in the different States. Membership was hereditary. The general and many of the state societies are still in existence. We give a list of members of the Massachusetts State Society, with their record, taken from the Society's late publication, who have descendants living and who lived themselves in Washington county:

BURNHAM, JOHN.—Born, Ipswich, Mass., 10 Dec., 1749; died Derry, N. H., 8 June, 1843; Lieut. in Little's Reg't, Bunker's Hill, Long Island, and Trenton; Captain 1 Jan. 1777, of light infantry in Brook's (8th) Reg't at Saratoga, Monmouth and Stony Point; served under LaFayette at the capture of the British redoubt at Yorktown, and promoted to Major 9 Jan. 1783. In 1790 he was one of the founders of Marietta, Ohio; he afterwards settled in Derry, N. H.

GOODALE, NATHAN.—Born, Brookfield, Mass., about 1743; killed by Indians near Belpre, O., Mch. 1793. Lieut. in J. Read's Reg't, 1775; Ass't Engineer to Col. Rufus Putnam at siege of Boston; Captain, 1 Jan. 1777, in Putnam's (5th) Reg't; present at capture of Burgoyne; wounded and made prisoner at Valentine's Hill, 1778. Captain Goodale performed much arduous and valuable service. He removed to Ohio in 1788; settled at Belpre in April, 1789; and took the lead in the defence of the settlement against the Indians.

HASKELL, JONATHAN.—Born, Rochester, Mass., 19 March, 1755; died, Belpre, Ohio, 11 Jan., 1817; Ensign and Adjutant in Bradford's (14th) Reg't, 31 Jan., 1777; Lieut., 4 Feb., 1779; Aide to Gen. Patterson, 1779; Lieutenant and Adjutant in Brook's (7th) Reg't 1782–83; appointed Captain 2d U. S. Infantry, 4 March, 1791; Major, 20 March, 1794; serving in Wayne's successful Indian campaign, Aug., 1794; emigrated in 1788 to Ohio, and left descendants in Washington county.

OLIVER, ROBERT.—Born, Boston, 1738; died Marietta, Ohio, May, 1810, removed to Barre while young; a teacher in 1775; Capt. in Doolittle's Reg't 12 June, 1775; at seige of Boston; Major in Greaton's (3d) Reg't, 1st Nov. 1777; Brigade-Major 1780; Brevet-Colonel 1782; distinguished at storming of Hessian entrenchments at Saratoga; Acting Adjutant General of Northern Army, and an excellent disciplinarian; one of the founders of Marietta, Ohio, in 1788. President of Territorial Council 1800–1803, and a Judge of Court of Common Pleas.

PUTNAM, RUFUS.—Born, Sutton, Mass., 9 April, 1738; died, Marietta, O., 4 May, 1824; a mill-right; a private soldier in the campaigns 1757–60, in Canada; then settled in New Braintree, Mass.; Lieut. Col. in D. Brewer's Reg't, May, 1775; employed as an engineer in constructing the seige-works around Boston; chief engineer of the defences of New York in 1776; Colonel 5 August, 1776, and commanded the 5th Reg't until Com. Brig.-General 7 Jan. 1783; distinguishing himself at Saratoga; Aide to Gen'l Lincoln, in quelling Shay's rebellion; one of the founders of Marietta, Ohio, in 1788; appointed a Judge of Northwestern Territory, 1789; re-appointed Brigadier General 4 May, 1792; U. S. Surveyor General 1793–1803; Member of Ohio Constitutional Convention, 1803.

RICE, OLIVER.—Born, Sudbury, Mass., 26th July, 1752; died Belpre, O.; Ensign in Wesson's (9th) Reg't, 1777; Lieut. 5th Sept., 1781, in H. Jackson's Reg't.; in the 4th Reg't in 1783; removed from Walpole, N. H., to Marietta, Ohio, about 1788.

SPROAT, EBENEZER.—Born, Middleborough, Mass., 1752; died, Marietta, Ohio, Feb'y, 1805; Major in Cotton's Reg't, May, 1775, at siege of Boston; in Frances' Reg't in 1776; Lieutenant Colonel 12th Reg't, 1 Jan. 1777; and 29 Sept., 1778, Lieutenant Colonel

Commanding in Glover's Brigade at Trenton, Princeton, and Monmouth; inspector of Brigade under Steuben; emigrated to Ohio in 1788, and called by the Indians, "the Big Buckeye;" Sheriff and Colonel of Militia.

STACY, WILLIAM.—Born, Salem, Mass.; died, Marietta, Ohio, 1804; removed to New Salem; led a Company to Cambridge, and made Major of Woodbridge's Reg't, May, 1775; in battle of Bunker's Hill; Lieut. Colonel of Shepperd's (4th) Reg't, 1 Jan. 1777; joined Alden's (12th) Reg't, and 11 Nov., 1778, was captured by Indians at Cherry Valley, N. Y., remaining four years a prisoner; Colonel of 2d Reg't in 1782; settled in Marietta, Ohio, in 1789; and left descendants in Washington County, Ohio.

TUPPER, ANSELM.—Son of Gen. Benjamin, born, Kingston, Mass.; died, Marietta, Ohio, 25 Dec. 1808; Lieut. in his father's (11th) Reg't, 26 Sept. 1780.

TUPPER, BENJAMIM.—Born, Houghton, Mass., 1738; died, Marietta, Ohio, June 1792; a soldier in the French War (1756–63); Major of Fellow's Reg't, May, 1775; at seige of Boston, where he distinguished himself; Lieut-Col. in Ward's Reg't, 4 Nov., 1775; Col. 11th Reg't, 7 July, 1777; 6th Reg't, 1783; present at Saratoga and Monmouth; Brevetted Brigadier-General, 1783; member of Massachusetts Legislature from Chesterfield, and active in suppressing Shay's Insurrection; settled in Ohio in 1788; one of the founders of Marietta in 1788, and a Judge.

BRADFORD, ROBERT.—Born at Plymouth, Mass., 1750; died at Belpre, Ohio, 1823; descended from Gov. William; Ensign in Bailey's (2d) regiment, 1775; Lieutenant, 1776; commissioned Captain, 21 June, 1779; served through the war from Bunker's Hill to Yorktown; brevetted Major in 1783; settled at Belpre, O., in 1789.

COOPER, EZEKIAL.—Of Danvers, Ensign in Hutchinson's regiment at siege of Boston; Lieutenant in Putnam's (5th) regiment, 1777–82; commissioned Captain in Sproat's (2d) regiment, 7 Jan., 1783; removed to Ohio in 1788; living at Warrentown, O., in 1807.

•CUSHING, NATHANIEL.—Born at Pembroke, Mass., 8 April, 1753; died at Marietta, Ohio, Aug., 1814; Lieutenant in Brewer's regiment at siege of Boston; Captain in Vose's (1st) regiment, 1 Jan., 1777; afterward in Putnam's (5th) regiment; Brigade Major, 1 Dec., 1781–83; surprised De Lancey's Loyalists Corps in May, 1780; and brevet Major in 1782; emigrated to Ohio in 1788; was one of the founders of Belpre in 1789.

KING, ZEBULON.—Born at Raynham, Mass., 16 Oct., 1750; Lieutenant in Bradford's (14th) regiment; commissioned Captain, 4 Oct., 1780; in Brooks' (7th) regiment in 1783; emigrated to Ohio after the war, and killed there by the Indians.

MILLS, WILLIAM.—Of Westminister, commissioned Ensign in Bradford's (14th) regiment, 31 Jan., 1777; Captain, 11 May, 1781; in Brooks' (7th) regiment in 1783; settled in Ohio in 1789.

SARGENT, WINTHROP.—Born at Gloucester, Mass., 1 May 1753; died at New Orleans, 3 June, 1820; Harvard University, 1771; entered the army in 1775; commissioned Captain Lieutenant in Knox's artillery 16 March, 1776; Captain in Crane's artillery, 1 Jan., 1777; present at Trenton and Brandywine; Aide to Gen. Howe and made Brevet Major; appointed Surveyor of North Western Territory, 1786; its Secretary, 1787; Governor 1798–1801; Adjutant General of St. Clair's army, and wounded on its defeat, 8 Nov., 1791; Adjutant and Inspector-General in Wayne's campaign, 1794–95; settled near Natchez, Miss.

STONE, JONATHAN.—Born at New Baintree, Mass., 1751; died in Belpre, Ohio, 25 March, 1801; Orderly Sergeant in Leonard's regiment at siege of Boston; Ensign and Lieutenant in Francis' regiment, 1776; Paymaster in Putnam's (5th) regiment, 1 Jan., 1777; Lieutenant 15th regiment, 1779; Captain 1779–83; in the battles with Burgoyne; went with Gen. R. Putnam as a surveyor to Ohio in 1786–87, and settled in 1789, near the mouth of the Little Kanawha, at Belpre, Ohio.

WHITE, HAFFIELD.—Born at Danvers; died about 1817, near Waterford, Ohio, where he left descendants; Lieutenant in Hutchinson's regiment at siege of Boston; commissioned Captain in Putnam's (5th) regiment, 1 Jan., 1777; served at Lexington, Trenton, Hubbardton, and Saratoga; emigrated to Ohio in Dec., 1787.

WILLIAMS, ABRAHAM.—Of Barnstable, emigrated to Ohio, and died about 1796; Lieutenant in Whitcomb's regiment, 1776; commissioned Captain in Sproat's (12th) regiment, 29 Sept., 1778; Brigade Major in 1783.